Too Much Mush!

Too Much Mush!

retold by Abby Levine

illustrated by Kathy Parkinson

ALBERT WHITMAN & COMPANY, Niles, Illinois

Text ©1989 by Abby Levine.
Illustrations ©1989 by Kathy Parkinson.
Published in 1989 by Albert Whitman & Company,
5747 West Howard Street, Niles, Illinois 60648.
Published simultaneously in Canada
by General Publishing Limited, Toronto.
All rights reserved.
Printed in the United States of America.
Type set in Veljovic Medium.
Designer: Karen Johnson Campbell
10   9   8   7   6   5   4   3   2   1

Library of Congress Cataloging-in-Publication Data

Levine, Abby.
Too much mush!

Summary: When they discover a magic pot that makes
mush on command, Hannah and her mother delight until the
word to make it stop is forgotten and the village is
flooded with mountains of mush.
[1. Fairy tales   2. Folklore—Germany]
I. Parkinson, Kathy, ill.   II. Title.
PZ8.L4788To   1989   398.2'1'0943   [E]   88-33906
ISBN 0-8075-8025-2

J
398.21

Between the black forest and the blue mountains lay a tiny village. Everyone there was poor, without enough to eat. Even the pigs and cows and chickens were thin.

Poorest of all were Hanna and her mother.

Each night, they dreamed of their favorite foods:

    peas and beets,
    roasted meats,
        bubbling beans,
      salad greens,
          cabbage rolls,
          doughnut holes,

    but—mostly—steaming mush in bowls!

One day, when there was nothing left to eat in their house,
Hanna went into the forest to search for food.

She roamed darker and deeper. She tripped over roots and

was scratched by brambles. But there were no fruits or nuts or
berries anywhere.

Suddenly she smelled a wonderful smell.

She followed it as if it were a road. The smell grew stronger and stronger. It was hot, steaming mush!

Sitting under a tree was an old woman. She was stirring a funny iron pot.

The old woman smiled. "I have been waiting for you, Hanna," she said. "This pot is yours. With it, you will never be hungry again."

She scooped out all the mush into a big wooden bowl.
"Cook, pot, cook!" she commanded. At once, the empty pot
began to fill with mush. Then the old woman said, "Cease,
pot, cease!" Instantly, the mush stopped rising.

"You must say the words exactly right," the old woman
warned. She lifted up the pot and put it in Hanna's arms. To
Hanna's amazement, it felt cool and light as a feather.
Hanna hurried home.

Now two happy people lived in the poor cottage. Whenever they were hungry, Hanna would say, "Cook, pot, cook!" And when the pot had made enough, she would say, "Cease, pot, cease!"

One morning, Hanna rose early to walk in the forest. Soon her mother got up. She stretched and yawned. Her stomach rumbled. Time for mush!

"Cook, pot, cook!" Hanna's mother ordered, and the pot began to fill.

"Stop, pot, stop!" her mother said. But the pot did not stop.
"Quit, pot, quit!" her mother called. But the pot did not quit.
"Oh dear! No more, pot! **HELP!**" shouted Hanna's mother.
"There's too much mush!"

The neighbors heard her cry, and they rushed in.
They yelled orders at the pot, but the pot cooked on.

It cooked through the morning and through the afternoon.
Mush filled the little house and oozed into the street.

It swelled higher and higher until it was everywhere.
There were slivers of mush, rivers of mush,

fountains of mush,
mountains of mush,

piles of mush,

miles of mush!

When Hanna returned, she saw at once what had happened.
She ran home as fast as she could lift her sticky feet.

"Cease, pot, cease!" she shouted. And in a moment,
the pot stopped.

Her mother hugged her. "Hanna, whatever would I do
without you?" she said.

Everyone came out with spoons and bowls and tubs.

They ate until they were full and carried more home.

From that day on, no one in the tiny village went hungry.
Sometimes they had a little mush.
Sometimes they had a lot of mush.

But never, ever again did they have
TOO MUCH MUSH!